PETIE'S FIRST HAIRCUT

Written by Kathy Joseph
Illustrated by Brett Thompson
Editorial development by friends and family
Visit us at www.glcalpacaplace

ISBN-13: 978-1979502092 International
ISBN-10: 1979502099 National

THIS BOOK BELONGS TO_____

Look for these words in the story:

alpaca
caretaker
catch pen
cria
fleece
halter
hum or hmmm
pronking
shear the white alpacas first
water trough

You can find them in the Glossary
in the back of the book.

CAST OF CHARACTERS

Belanca

Cory

Danny

Gabe

Grayson

Hannah

Mosey

Petie

Victoria

Grayson yawned his first words of the day, "What a great morning! Hmmmm. The air is fresh. There is a little breeze, and the sky is blue."

"I couldn't agree with you more," Gabe hummed. "I can hardly wait to get out in the pasture and graze in the shade under that big elm tree."

1

"You mean you are not going to play with us? I feel so good today that I was hoping to do some pronking before it gets too hot," hummed Petie.

"You crias are just going to have to play without me until shearing day. It is too hot for pronking if you are carrying around this heavy, black fleece. I am heading for the shade," said Gabe.

2

"Yeah, it sure has warmed up lately," replied Danny. "It must be getting close to shearing day."

"Shearing day? What's shearing day?" questioned Petie.

Seeing an opportunity to have some fun with the crias, who had never experienced a shearing, Gabe cleared his throat and with a chuckle he answered, "Well Petie, once a year we all get these really great haircuts. They make us look so different that our friends don't even recognize us."

Confused and scared, Petie was barely able to stutter, "Rrr...Rrr...Really?"

"Oh Gabe," Danny laughed and turned his attention to Petie. "It's not that bad. Actually, it feels really good and is so much more comfortable for the hot summer months that lie ahead. It is easier to feel the cool water against your skin when we get a shower from the hose."

"The part I like most is when we take a dirt bath after the shower. It is like getting to scratch an itch that is all over your body," hummed Belanca.
"Frankly, I love shearing day," Victoria interrupted.
"At least once a year I can do something with these bangs."

"I am not so sure about this," said Petie fidgeting nervously. "I like the way I look. My long, silky fleece makes me one of the favorites."

"Look! Here they come!" cried Danny.

"Who's coming?" asked Hannah.

"The people who shear us," answered Gabe.

6

Instantly, all the alpacas turned to watch a blue SUV pull into the driveway. Then Petie called out, "Quick! Have Danny stand in the doorway so they can't get through the gate."

Victoria laughed, her bangs blowing in the breeze, "Oh Petie, that only works on alpacas, not humans. Danny won't be able to keep anyone out of the corral. Relax, it will be okay."

"Personally, I think it will be fun to have a new hairdo. I wonder what is 'in' this year," Hannah thought out loud.

"Yeah," added Mosey. "I wouldn't mind having a little fluff taken off the sides."

9

The alpacas watched all of the commotion near the garage where the shearing would take place. After everything was set up, their caretaker started walking towards the corral with the halter and lead rope.

10

"Well, I'll tell you one thing," declared Petie,
"I'm not going first."

"Think again," said Gabe. Every year they
shear the white alpacas first."

"Why is that?" questioned Grayson.

Victoria responded, "I am sure that it is because the dark
colors, especially the black alpacas, are the prettiest and they want to
save the best for last."

"Yeah, right," Belanca added sarcastically, shaking her head. Turning to the crias, she said, "I don't know why, but they always start with the white crias, go through the different colors from light to dark and end with the black alpacas."

"Exactly what I said," Victoria added.

Everyone just looked at Victoria, smiled and all together replied, "Right!"

12

The caretaker with the halter had now reached the corral.
She came in and started walking toward Petie.

"Can't catch me!" Petie called, and he began running
around the corral. The caretaker just kept
moving toward Petie, who proudly called
over his shoulder, "Hmmmm, too fast
for you, huh?"

Because Petie was watching over his shoulder, he didn't realize that he was running right into the catch pen. The caretaker simply closed the gate and Petie realized that he was trapped.

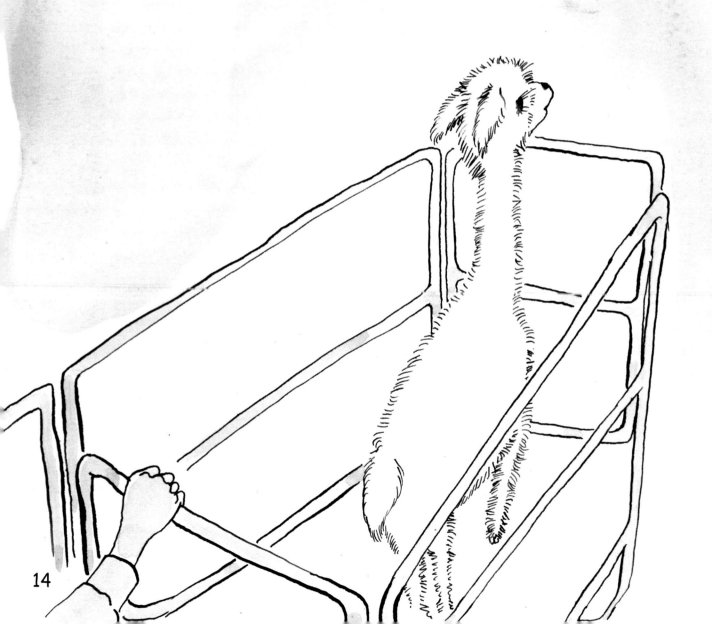

Gently, the caretaker slipped the halter over Petie's head and
led him out of the corral.

"Hey you guys, help me. I don't want a haircut!" called Petie as
he was led toward the garage.

"Hang in there Petie," Hannah called back to him. "You'll be fine.
It will be okay!"

15

Petie disappeared into the garage. Ten minutes later he emerged with a new, short haircut. As Petie was led back to the corral, Cory asked the other alpacas, "Who is that alpaca and what happened to Petie?"

"That **is** Petie," said Danny. "That is Petie after being shorn."

"No way!" said Cory. "He looks so different."

"Trust me," Danny replied. "Give him a sniff when he gets back and you'll see."

So when Petie came back into the corral, all the crias ran up and sniffed him all over. "That is him!" announced Hannah to the rest of the herd.

"This is so embarrassing," mumbled Petie.

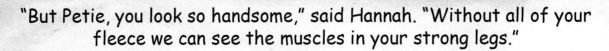

"But Petie, you look so handsome," said Hannah. "Without all of your fleece we can see the muscles in your strong legs."

Petie puffed up with pride when he saw Hannah batting her eyelashes at him and replied, "I do?"

"HmmmHmmm," hummed Hannah.

18

Petie blushed from the special attention.

When the caretaker turned to find another alpaca to shear, Hannah cried out, "Take me next; take me! Can we request special haircuts? I want one of those pretty, fancy hairdos."

Belanca just smiled and said, "Hannah, you'll have to wait your turn. Remember, they do all of the white alpacas first and then move to the darker colors. You won't have to wait long because you are a light fawn color. And no, you can't have a special hairdo."

"Oh, all right," said Hannah. "I guess I can wait my turn."

It wasn't long before they came for Hannah. She was so excited. You could hear her giggling from the garage all the way to the corral during her shearing. "Hmmmmm, that tickles. Cut it out! Hee, hee, hee! Now what are you doing? Oh, you are cutting my toenails. No one said that I would get a pedicure too. This is awesome. It is like an alpaca day at the spa."

When she was finished, Hannah was able to see her reflection in the van window. She was so happy with her new look that she strutted all the way back to the corral and went right up to Petie hoping for a compliment. But instead she found Petie admiring his own reflection in the water trough.

Hannah started laughing. "I thought you didn't want a haircut," she reminded him.

"Okay, okay," laughed Petie. "I guess I did overreact a little. Shearing day isn't so bad after all. It will definitely make the summer more fun."

One by one the alpacas went into the garage in full fleece and came back with their annual haircuts, feeling much cooler and ready for summer.

24

"Look!" cried Cory. "Here she comes with the hose for our shower."

All the alpacas ran to the hose and danced in the stream of water, each trying to get in front of the others.

As soon as they were finished playing in the water, the alpacas ran to the dirt bathtubs and rolled in the lose dirt until they were covered in mud.

When the fun was over, Petie looked at Hannah and the other dirty alpacas with their new haircuts. He nodded his head and admitted, "I guess there was nothing to be afraid of. Next time I am going to be brave when I have to try something new. Shearing day is the best. I can hardly wait for next year!"

Alpaca Glossary

alpaca

These gentle animals came to the U.S. from South America. They are cousins to llamas and camels and are raised for their fabulous wool.

caretaker

This term refers to the human(s) that are responsible for taking care of the alpacas on a daily basis.

catch pen

This is a small fenced-in area usually found inside the corral which is used to catch the alpacas.

cria

This is what we call a baby or young alpaca.

fleece

Alpaca fleece is the natural fiber shorn from an alpaca. While it is similar to sheep's wool, it is stronger, warmer, not prickly, and has no lanolin (wool grease), which makes it better for people with allergies. It is used to make a variety of products like hats, gloves, sweaters and even rugs.

halter

A halter is a rope or strap with a loop placed around the alpaca's head - used for walking the alpaca.

hum or hmmm

Known as humming, it is the sound alpacas use to communicate.

pronking

Alpacas leap in the air with an arched back and stiff legs. They usually do this when they are happy or playing.

shear the white alpacas first

In order to keep all of the colors separated, the common practice in alpaca shearing is to start with the white alpacas and move through the colors from light to dark. This way the different colors won't get mixed together.

water trough

This is a large container which holds water for the alpacas to drink.

Cast of Characters

Belanca

Cory

Danny

Gabe

Grayson

Hannah

Mosey

Petie

Victoria

About the Author

Kathy Joseph is a retired band director who fell in love with alpacas and began raising
them for her future retirement hobby. She lives in Grand Junction, Colorado,
with her alpaca family. Spending the past 15 years with these amazing
animals has brought great joy into her life. In the summer of 2017 she completed her first book, *Danny's in
the Doorway* which was inspired by Danny, the alpaca standing and blocking the
gateway into the pasture. Kathy's realization that the alpacas had a lot to say
about life lessons along with the first book's success inspired her to write a second book.

About the Illustrator

Brett Thompson has been drawing and painting since he was just a little boy. He has lived in
Rifle, Colorado; NYC; Tokyo, Japan; Las Cruces, NM and currently resides in Grand Junction, Colorado,
drawing characters in all the various places he has lived.

Life with Petie the Alpaca Series

Made in the USA
San Bernardino, CA
16 April 2018